ABOUT THE BANK STREET READY-TO-READ SERIES

Seventy-five years of educational research and innovative teaching have given the Bank Street College of Education the reputation as America's most trusted name in early childhood education.

Because no two children are exactly alike in their development, we have designed the *Bank Street Ready-to-Read* series in three levels to accommodate the individual stages of reading readiness of children ages four through eight.

- ● *Level 1:* GETTING READY TO READ—read-alouds for children who are taking their first steps toward reading.

- ● *Level 2:* READING TOGETHER—for children who are just beginning to read by themselves but may need a little help.

- ○ *Level 3:* I CAN READ IT MYSELF—for children who can read independently.

Our three levels make it easy to select the books most appropriate for a child's development and enable him or her to grow with the series step by step. The *Bank Street Ready-to-Read* books also overlap and reinforce each other, further encouraging the reading process.

We feel that making reading fun and enjoyable is the single most important thing that you can do to help children become good readers. And we hope you'll be a part of Bank Street's long tradition of learning through sharing.

The Bank Street College of Education

To Beth, Dave, and Allison
—J.O.
For Connor
—K.O.

ROW, ROW, ROW YOUR BOAT

A Bantam Book/November 1993

Published by Bantam Doubleday Dell Books for Young Readers,
a division of Bantam Doubleday Dell Publishing Group, Inc.
1540 Broadway, New York, New York 10036

Series graphic design by Alex Jay/Studio J

Special thanks to James A. Levine, Betsy Gould,
Diane Arico, and Melissa Turk.

The trademarks "Bantam Books" and the portrayal of a rooster
are registered in the U.S. Patent and Trademark Office and in
other countries. Marca Registrada.

Library of Congress Cataloging-in-Publication Data
Oppenheim, Joanne.
Row, row, row your boat / by Joanne Oppenheim ; illustrated by
Kevin O'Malley.
p.   cm.—*(Bank Street ready-to-read)*
"A Byron Preiss book."
"A Bantam book."
Summary: While singing "Row, Row, Row Your Boat"
in the bathtub, a boy becomes the skipper
of several imaginary vessels.
ISBN 0-553-09498-X.—ISBN 0-553-37193-2 (pbk.)
1. Children's songs—Texts. [1. Boats—Songs and music.
2. Songs.] I. O'Malley, Kevin, 1961– ill. II. Title.
III. Series.
PZ8.3.O615Ro   1993
782.42164'0268—dc20   92-29015   CIP   AC

Published simultaneously in the United States and Canada
PRINTED IN THE UNITED STATES OF AMERICA

0 9 8 7 6 5 4 3 2 1

Row, Row, Row Your Boat

by Joanne Oppenheim
Illustrated by Kevin O'Malley

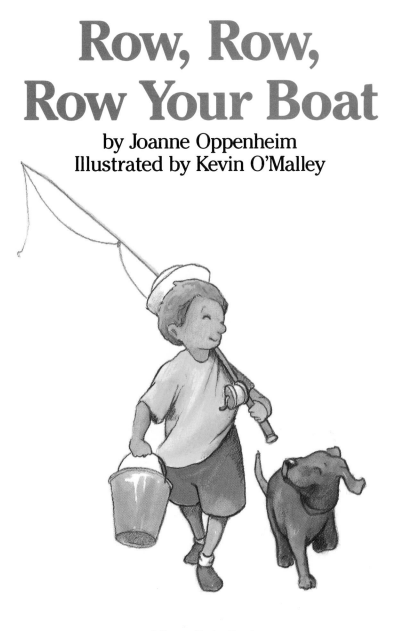

A Byron Preiss Book

A BANTAM BOOK

4

Row, row, row your boat
gently down the stream.

Merrily, merrily, merrily, merrily,
life is but a dream.

8

Sail, sail, sail your boat,
sail across the bay.
A gusty wind will fill the sail
and take you on your way.

9

Paddle left, then paddle right,
paddle side to side.
Whatever you do,
don't tip the canoe!
Just paddle yourself a ride.

Drift, drift, drift along,
like clouds up in the sky.
Go gliding on a river raft,
and watch the world go by.

Rev, rev, rev your boat,
go racing on the lake.
Vroom! Vroom! the motor roars
and churns a wavy wake.

15

Back and forth and back again,
the ferry takes your car.
Across the river and back again,
ferries don't go far.

Toot! Toot! calls the tug
as it shoves the ship.
Hoot! Hoot! the ship replies
as it leaves the slip.

Pull, pull, pull the barge,
move a heavy load.
Pull, pull, watch the wake
on the river road.

Load, load, load the freight,
fill the hold below.
From truck to train
to shipping lane,
that's how the cargo goes.

Hoot! Hoot! the fireboat hoots,
its hoses spray and spout.
Hear the captain shout out loud,
"Put this fire out!"

26

Cast, cast, cast your line,
sink your line and hook.
All aboard a fishing boat,
catch some fish to cook.

Dive, dive, dive your boat,
go diving down below.
Your submarine
can dive down deep,
way down where fishes glow.

29

See, see the city sights,
buildings built so tall.
Uptown, downtown,
crosstown too—
we'll try to see it all!

Row, row, row your boat
gently down the stream.
Merrily, merrily, merrily, merrily,
life is but a dream.